HEAVEN IN T

By Lucias McCullough

Back Cover Summary

In the restless heart of Clarendon, Arkansas, where Ambition burns as hot as betrayal, three lives collide in a storm of passion and danger.

Andre Lamar, a gifted musician, singer, and poet, performs with a soul so raw that his words cut deeper than knives. His rising career has begun to draw crowds - but noting prepares him for the moment he lays eyes on **Tiffani Rhodes**, a successful boutique owner whose elegance and independance hides wounds she never speaks of.

Andre's best friend, Kashaka, has harbored a secret obsession with Tiffani for years. Though he smiles in Andre's face, jealousy coils silently inside him like a venomous snake. When Tiffani unexpectedly finds herself drawn into Andre's world- captivated by his presence, his talent, and his ability to read her heart like a page in his notebook - Kashaka's envy turns into something far darker.

As Andre and Tiffani's passion ignites, Kashaka's quiet resentment erupts into violence. He kidnaps Tiffani, dragging her to a hidden warehouse in the city's shadows. Andre races against time, risking everything to find her.
But to bring Tiffani home, Andre must face the man he once called brother - in a brutal showdown that could shatter every bond he ever trusted.

Love brought them together.
Obsession tore them apart.
Only blood and fire will decide who survives.
HEAVEN IN THE CROSSFIRE

The first book of the "Crossfire" Series

By Lucias McCullough

Cover design and interior layout: Lucias McCullough

Dedication

This book is dedicated to everyone who has survived the trials of "Love". It is dedicated to all those who have braved the flames of unbridled passion, the intrigue of infatuation, the despair of the imperfections of unexpected attraction and the engulfing waters of affection.

For Clarendon, Arkansas - The city that watered my roots and cultivated me to grow into my future.

Special Dedication to my brother Timmy Burks - Til' we meet again.

Copyright Page

2025 Lucias McCullough. All Rights Reserved.

No Part of this publication may be reproduced, stored, or

transmitted in any for or by any means - electronic, mechanical, photocopying,

recording, or otherwise without prior written permission form the author.

This is a work of fiction. Names, characters, places and incidents are either products of the author's imagination or used fictitiously. Any resemblance to actual persons, living or deceased or actual events is purely coincidental.

Printed in the United States of America

First Edition, 2025

About the Author

Lucias McCullough is a storyteller drawn to the raw spaces where love, loyalty, ambition, and betrayal collide. With a voice rooted in realism and emotion, he writes characters who feel "lived in"- flawed, passionate, and searching for meaning in a world that rarely shows mercy.

Blending elements of **romance, street drama, and suspense**, Lucias explores the thin line between devotion and obsession, and the price people pay when love and jealousy cross paths. His stories are grounded in authentic human emotion, inspired by real-life struggles, resilience, and the unspoken battles people carry everyday.

Heaven in the crossfire is his debut novel, marking the beginning of a body of work focused on intense relationships, hard choices, and the power of love to both save and destroy. Through vivid imagery and emotionally charged storytelling, Lucias invites readers into worlds where hearts are tested, loyalty is questioned, and survival often depends on the strength to face the fire.

When not writing, Lucias continues to develop creative projects that blend art, music, and visual storytelling - always driven by the belief that the most powerful stories are the ones that tell the truth.

Table of Contents

Heaven in the Crossfire

The first book of the "Crossfire" series

Dedication

Copyright

About the Author

Chapter One - The Man with Music in his veins

Chapter Two - Accidental Collisions

Chapter Three - Fate has a favorite target

Chapter Four - Sparks and Shadows

Chapter Five - The poem that broke the night open

Chapter Six - A man becoming a threat

Chapter Seven - The city without her

Chapter Eight - Hunting in the dark

Chapter Nine - Brothers turned Enemies

CHAPTER ONE - THE MAN WITH MUSIC IN HIS VEINS

The lights inside The Starlight Club were dim, washed in a purple glow that made shadows dance across the walls. Soft conversations drifted through the air like smoke. Tonight's open mic was packed - local artists, poets, singers, hustlers, suits, dreamers, and the heartbroken all sat shoulder to shoulder, wating for someone to spill their soul on stage

Andre Lamar stood behind the curtain, adjusting the mic in his hand. He wasn't nervous - he never got nervous. Not when he had words ready to pour out of him. He lived for this. Music wasn't talent for him; it was blood, bone, breath. It was everything.

But tonight felt different.

He kept feeling a pull, a strange sense that someone out there was about to change his life.

"Yo, you ready?" came a voice behind him.

Andre turned to see Kashaka, his childhood friend and right hand. Kashaka wore a faded denim jacket, hood halfway up, his eyes dark and sharp as always. He smirked and gave Andre a hard pat on the shoulder.

"You bout to kill it tonight," Kashaka said. "Crowd's hungry."

Andre nodded. "Always"

But Kashaka wasn't really looking at him. His gaze drifted toward the audience, searching for someone.

Andre stepped out onto the stage. The crowd clapped. Some cheered. A few called his name. He tapped the mic twice, testing the echo.

Then he saw her.

Tiffani.

She sat near the back in a sleek white jumpsuit, legs crossed, neck long and graceful, eyes like warm honey even from across the room. She didn't smile. Didn't fidget. She watched the stage with the calm confidence of a woman who'd seen enough of life to not be impressed easily.

Andre felt the breath catch in his chest.

For a moment, everything else blurred.

He didn't know her name yet. Didn't know her story. But something about her presence lit a fuse inside him.

He began his piece.

A slow rhythmic vocal flowed from his lips, a spoken-word cadence that held the room in its grip.

"You ever met someone…
and suddenly your heartbeat starts speakin' in
new languages?
Like it's been waitin' for that one face,
that one moment… to rewrite your whole
alphabet?"

Some people snapped. Others leaned forward.

But he wasn't performing for the room anymore. He was performing for her.

Tiffani didn't react - not at first. She stared, expression unreadable, as if analyzing the architecture of his voice.

Andre smiled inwardly. She was the type that didn't fall easy.

Exactly his favorite kind.

When he finished, the applause rose like thunder. Andre bowed his head in thanks, but his eyes went back to the woman in white.

She was already slipping out of her seat.

Walking away.

Disappearing in the night.

Backstage, Andre was still replaying her face in his mind when Kashaka walked up beside him, arms folded.

"You see her?" Kashaka asked casually.

Andre raised an eyebrow. "Who?"

"That woman you were staring at the whole damn performance."

Andre tried to not show his surprise. "She fine. I'll give you that."

Kashaka's jaw tightened - just a little. Almost invisible.

"Her name's Tiffani," he said slowly. "I've known her for years."

Andre blinked. "You know her?"

"Yeah." Kashaka's eyes hardened, just for a second. "Real well, actually."

Andre didn't notice the shift. Didn't see the spark of jealousy ignite. He just laughed softly.

"You should introduce us sometime."

Kashaka didn't laugh back.

"I'll think about it," he said.

CHAPTER TWO - ACCIDENTAL COLLISIONS

Rain had settled over Clarendon like a soft, steady heartbeat.

The kind that made the streets shine and the neon lights blur into streaks of color. Tiffani walked briskly down Madison Avenue, clutching

a thin umbrella, the night's cool breath brushing against her skin.

She wasn't thinking about the man on stage from earlier.

At least, thats what she told herself.

She had only stopped by The Starlight Club to clear her mind - business had been ruthless lately, employees quitting, venders playing games,

rent increasing. Entrepreneurship was glamor only for people

who never lived inside it.

Still…

there had been something in Andre's voice. Something unsettling. Something she didn't want to think about.

She shook it off.

Her Boutique, **Tiffani Monroe Designs**, stood on the corner - modern glass windows, gold lettering, mannequins dressed in bold, artistic fashions she personally curated. It was her sanctuary. Her empire.

She reached the door, pulled out her key… and froze.

Someone was standing under the awning.

A tall figure. Hood up. Hands in pockets.

"Relax - its just me."

Tiffani exhaled in relief as Kashaka stepped into the light.

"Kash, You scared the hell out of me," she said, pushing open the door.

"My bad." He smirked a little. "Didn't wanna stand in the rain."

Kashaka followed her inside, glancing like he was inspecting the space - even though he'd been there plenty of times before.

They had history, though never romantic. Kashaka had always hinted, always lingered a little too long when they hugged, but she's never given him a reason to think she wanted more.

He never stopped hoping anyway.

"How'd the event go tonight?" she asked, setting her purse behind the counter.

"Same as usual." Kashaka shrugged. "Crowd was loud. Andre did his thing."

Tiffani hesitated.

She hadn't planned to mention this part. Not at all.

But the memory of Andre's words - the way he delivered them like he was pulling truth out of her chest - lingered like smoke in her thoughts.

"He's talented," she said cautiously.

Kashaka's eyes snapped to her.

"You talked to him?"

"No. I left right after his piece."

Kashaka stared at her for a beat too long - an unspoken warning behind his casual expression.

"He notices women staring at him," Kashaka muttered. "Don't give him a big head."

Tiffani laughed lightly. "Who said I was staring? He just caught my attention, that's all. He's… different.

That did it. Kashaka's smile shattered. He looked away, jaw tightening.

"He aint what you think," he said under his breath.

Tiffani frowned. "What's that supposed to mean?"

Before he could answer, the boutique door slammed open - a gust of wind and rain sweeping in with a tall silhouette holding a soaked notebook over his head.

Tiffani's breath stalled.

Andre.

He was drenched, hoodie darkened by the rain, curls dripping over his forehead, chest rising with quick breaths as if he jogged the whole block.

"I'm -"   He caught sight of Kashaka. "Oh Kash, you here."

Kashaka didn't move. "What you doing at her store, bro?"

Andre lifted his notebook. "Dropped this earlier near the curb. I think somebody kicked it, rolled right under the door."

Tiffani blinked. "Wait - this is yours?"

She bent down to pick up the wet notebook lying near the mat. The cover was worn leather, pages slightly bent. Something compelled her to open it.

The first page held short lines of poetry - messy handwriting, but powerful.

"I don't chase dreams.

They chase me,

begging to be written

before the sun kisses the sky."

Tiffani's chest fluttered.

Andre rubbed the back of his neck. "Yeah… that's one of my old books. If its ruined, I'm screwed. There's like years of stuff in there-"

"Its beautiful," She said softly.

Kashaka's expression darkened instantly.

"So you just lettin' random strangers read your personal writings now?" Kashaka snapped at Andre.

Andre raised an eyebrow. "She ain't random."

Tiffani's pulse kicked.

She felt something - bold, reckless - rise inside her. She walked toward Andre, handing him the notebook gently.

"You should be more careful," she said with a small smile. "Words like those… they mean something."

Andre looked at her for a long moment. His voice lowered.

"Yeah. They do."

Silence pulled tight between them - warm, magnetic, electric.

Kashaka stepped forward abruptly.

"Alright," he said sharply. "Its late. We leaving."

"I didn't ask you to -" Tiffani began.

But she didn't finish.

Because Andre spoke at the same time.

"I was actually gonna walk her to her car."

Kashaka's head snapped toward him. "You what?"

Andre shrugged casually - but his eyes stayed on Tiffani. "Rain's getting pretty heavy. Thought it'd be the respectful thing."

Tiffani's pulse fluttered again - shocked by how simply Andre said it.

Kashaka stepped between them.

"She don't need help," he hissed.

"Its okay," Tiffani interrupted, grabbing her keys. "I'll walk out with both of you."

She closed the boutique, rain misting her face as they stepped outside. Kashaka walked stiffly on her right. Andre walked quietly on her left. Thunder rumbled in the distance.

As they reached her car, she turned to Andre.

"Thank you," she said softly.

He smiled - slow, confident, warm. "Anytime."

Kashaka glared at him from behind Tiffani's shoulder.

Andre didn't blink.

CHAPTER THREE - FATE HAS A FAVORITE TARGET

The next morning, sunlight crept through the blinds of Andre's one bedroom apartment. The place was humble - vinyl records stacked on shelves, notebooks scattered across the coffee table, a guitar leaning in the corner like a loyal friend. Music hummed quietly from his speakers, a mellow instrumental he'd been working on for weeks.

But he wasn't thinking about music.

He was thinking abou her.

Tiffani.

They way she looked at him last night - curious, cautious, drawn even when she tried not to be. He felt a pull he couldn't explain. It wasn't lust. It wasn't infatuation.

It was something that made the world around him shift.

His phone vibrated.

Kashaka.

Andre sighed and answered. "Yo."

"You busy?" Kashaka's voice was stiff.

"Nah. What's up?"

"You wanna hit the gym? Run some drills?"

Andre stretched, cracking his knuckles. "Yeah, cool. Meet you there in twenty."

But something in Kashaka's tone felt… off. Heavy.
Like a storm waiting on the horizon.

At the Gym

Sweat, rubber mats, the clank of weights - their usual spot. Kashaka worked the punching bag like he had demons to knock loose. Andre shadowboxed beside him, glancing over occasionally.

"You good bro?" Andre asked.

"Yeah, why wouldn't I be?"

Andre shrugged. "You just seem tense."

Kashaka hit the bag harder. "Just tired."

Andre didn't push it. He knew Kash had a past full of shadows - family trouble, street drama, things he never talked about unless he was drunk or angry.

But today's tension felt different.

Sharper.

"Listen, "he said without looking at Andre. "About last night…"

Andre waited.

"You don't wanna… mess around with her."
Kashaka muttered. "Trust me."

Andre blinked. "Why not?"

"Because I said so."

Andre stared at him. "Bro, she grown. She her own woman. What's the problem?"

Kashaka turned, eyes finally meeting his - dark and hostile.

"You always get everything, Dre. Everybody loves you. You walk in a room and women just - " He cut himself off, breathing hard. "Just leave her alone."

Andre stepped back, surprised. "You feelin' some type of way, Kash?

"No"

But his jaw was clenched.

His fist were shaking.

Andre shook his head. "Look, man… if you like her, just say that."

"I don't gotta explain nothin' to you."

Andre exhaled slowly. He's known Kash all his like - his moods, his pride, his sensitivity when it came to anything that felt like competition.

But this…
This was someting else.

Something dangerous.

Meanwhile - Across Town

Tiffani stood inside her boutique, rearranging a display of luxury handbags as customers trickled in and out. She wore tailored black slacks, a silk top and her hair pinned in a sleek updo.

But even surrounded by fashion, sales, and the comfort of her success…

Her mind drifted back to Andre.

To the way he spoke. The gentleness despite the power in his voice. The way his eyes studied her without trying to own her.

It unsettled her.

It intrigued her more than she cared to admit.

Her assistant, Maya, poked her head out from the back office.

"You keep sighing," Maya teased. "Either business stressing you or a man stressing you."

Tiffani rolled her eyes. "Nobody is stressing me."

Maya grinned. "Mmhmm. What happened? You met someone last night?"

"NO."

"Yes."

Tiffani groaned. "I mean - I met a man. But nothing happened."

"Is he cute?"

"He's…"

Her mind flashed back to Andre's rain-soaked hoodie, the soft smile, the confidence without arrogance.

"He's dangerous," she said finally.

"Ooooh. I see what's going on. " Maya laughed. "You're catching feelings."

"No. I'm catching curiosity. Big difference."

Maya shook her head. "Girl, life is short. If he's fine and respects you? Enjoy him."

Tiffani smirked. "I didn't say I wanted to enjoy him."

"You didn't have to. Your face said everything."

Before Tiffani could argue, the bell over the boutique door chimed.

Customers walked in.

No - Not customers.

Andre.

Standing in the doorway in a clean white tee, fresh-cut jeans, and a notebook tucked under his arm. The moment their eyes met, her heartbeat slipped out of rhythm.

"Oh," she breathed.

Maya glanced between them grinning like she'd been waiting for this exact moment. "I'm gon go organize something in the back.."

She vanished.

Andre stepped forward, smile warm but respectful.

"Hope I'm not bothering you," he said. "I was in the neighboorhood and figured I'd check if my notebook survived the rain."

Tiffani nodded toward the counter. "It dried fine. I kept it safe."

Andre chuckled. "Appreciate you."

There was a pause - soft magnetic.

Can I see your boutique?" he asked. Like… the way you see it? What you proud of?"

Tiffani blinked. No man had ever asked that. Not genuinely. Not without ulterior motives.

She found herself smiling.

"Sure," she said. "Come On."

She walked him through the store - fabrics she designed, pieces inspired by her childhood, displays arranged with intention.

Andre listened. Really listened.

"You're an artist," he murmured. "Just like me."

Her cheeks warmed. "I just love what I do."

"Yeah," he said softly. "I can tell."

Silence fell again - but this time it wasn't awkward.

It was charged.

Beautiful.

Dangerous.

Then Andre leaned in slightly, his voice lower.

"Tiffani… do you believe the universe puts people in each other's path on purpose?"

She swallowed. "Sometimes."

"Maybe this is one of those times."

Her breath caught.

But before she could respond, her phone buzzed violently.

a text.

Kashaka:

"Where you at?"

Another message came right after.

"*You alone?"

Tiffani's stomach tightened.

Andre noticed her expression change. "Everything okay?"

"Yeah… it's just -"
She hesitated.
"Its Kash."

Andre exhaled softly. "Right."

Their eyes met.

Both feeling something deepen - something neither of them could stop.

Something Kashaka would never allow.

CHAPTER FOUR - SPARKS AND SHADOWS

Night fell over Clarendon with a slow, simmering heat - the kind that made the air feel alive. Neon lights flickered down downtown streets, cars rolled by with heavy bass thumping from open windows, and the pulse of the city beat loud enough to drown out doubt… unless you carried doubt inside you.

Andre walked down the sidewalk toward The Elevations Lounge, a small, intimate venue where he'd been invited to perform an accoustic set. His guitar hung across his back, notebook in hand, thoughts tangled between excitement and hesitation.

Today had done something to him.

Seeing Tiffani in her boutique. Hearing her voice soften when she explained her designs. Watching her eyes glow at his attention. He couldn't get her out of his mind. But Kashaka's face… the tension in his voice… the warnings…

that couldn't be ignored either.

As Andre reached the venue, he took a breath and tried to center himself. He had a show to perform. He had an audience waiting. Music always settled him - it reminded him who he was, even when life tried to scatter the pieces.

Inside, the lounge buzzed with warm chatter. Small tables sat beneath golden lights. The crowd looked classy but relaxed. Andre checked in with the host tuning his guitar as people filled the room.

But outside…

Someone else was arriving too.

Tiffani in the Night

She didn't plan on coming. She didn't even know why she was here. Tiffani leaned against her car door for a moment after parking near Elevations, touching up her lipstick in the mirror. Her outfit was soft but elegant - deep burgundy dress, hair glowing in long curls. She told herself she only came because Maya insisted she needed a night out.

But she knew that was a lie.

Something in Andre's voice from earlier still echoed in her. "Maybe this is one of those times." The universe didn't place people in her path often. She had learned to build walls - big ones - after a lifetime of failed promises and

predatory men pretending to love her ambition. But Andre… He didn't want anything from her. He just saw her. And that scared her more than anything.

She stepped out of the car and walked toward the lounge. She didn't see the figure leaning against a parked SUV across the street. Watching her. Kashaka's jaw clenched as he followed her with his eyes. "So this how it is…" he muttered under his breath. His voice was almost a growl.

Inside - Two Worlds Colide Again

The lights dimmed. Conversations softened. Andre stepped onto the stage with calm confidence, lightly strumming the guitar.

The crowd leaned in.

He began with a smooth melodic riff, voice warm and deep.

"Sometimes a stranger can feel like

  a chapter you ain't read yet…

but somehow missed."

People swayed. Glasses clinked. A few women up front exchanged looks,, whispering about how fine he was. Andre glanced across the room-

- and froze.

Tiffani stood near the bar, eyes on him, lips slightly parted. Her presence pulled the air from his lungs. He kept singing, but the words changed- flowing, shifting, becoming someting raw.

"If I call you Heaven,

It ain't cause you perfect…

It's because you the first light I've seen

In a long, dark road."

Tiffani's heartbeat stumbled.

The line wasn't planned. He improvised it right there. For her. To her. The room faded away. Only they existed. When the song ended, the crowd erupted in applause, but Andre barely heard it. He set his guitar aside and walked into the audience.

Straight toward her. Tiffani exhaled softly. "You're… incredible."

"You came," he said, stepping closer.

"I didn't plan to."

"I'm glad you did."

Her lips curved slightly. "Why?"

"Because I wanted to see you again."

Silence wrapped around them, thick, warm, undeniable. She felt herself leaning in without moving. Andre's scent, his calm energy, his eyes that studied her like she was the last poem he'd ever write…

It was too much.

Too real.

Before she could answer, the lounge door swung open hard enough to rattle everyone.

Kashaka stormed inside.

His eyes locked on Tiffani.

Then Andre.

Then the space between them.

He clenched his fists.

"Oh hell no," he breathed.

Tiffani Stiffened. "Kash, what are you-"

"You left me on read," he snapped. "Now I know why."

Andre stepped forward, voice steady. "Chill, bro.

We just talking."

Kashaka jabbed a finger in his face. "Stay out of this."

"Nah," Andre said calmly. " I'm already in it."

Tiffany moved between them.

"This is not the place."

Kashaka looked at her, anger dissolving into something more painful.

More desperate.

"I been there for you for years, "he whispered harshly. "I protected you… loved you from a distance. And you choosing him?"

Tiffani swallowed hard. "Kash"… "you knew my boundaries. I never led you on."

"That don't matter!" he yelled, voice cracking.

"You supposed to be mine."

Andre's expression darkened.

"Watch yourself."

Kashaka turned, eyes burning.

"You think you better than me? You think you deserve her?"

Andre didn't flinch.

"I think she deserves to choose for herself."

   Murmurs spread through the lounge. People stared. A bartender reached for his phone in case he needed to called security.

Kashaka's breathing grew ragged - betraying the storm inside him.

"I ain't losing you," he whispered. "Not this time."

He backed away slowly - eyes locked on both of them, filled with a hatred neither of them recognized.

Then he walked out.

Silence dropped heavy as stone.

Tiffani pressed a trembling hard to her forehead. "I didn't know he felt that deeply…"

Andre stepped beside her. "His feelings ain't your fault."

"But he's your best friend…"

Andre paused, sadness flickering in his eyes. "He used to be."

Tiffani looked up at him, guilt and fear tangled together. " I don't want to be the reason you two are falling out."

"You're not."
He reached out and gently touched her hand.
"He made his choice. And I'm makin' mine."

Their fingers intertwined - softly, naturally.

And for the first time, Tiffani didn't pull away.

CHAPTER FIVE - THE POEM THAT BROKE THE NIGHT OPEN

The rest of the evening at The Elevations Lounge blurred into quiet murmurs and fading music. The confrontation with Kashaka left an invisible weight hanging in the air - but at the moment Tiffani and Andre stepped outside, the city felt different.

Larger.
Quieter.
Charged.

A thin breeze brushed between them as they walked down the sidewalk, neither speaking at first. The streetlights painted long shadows across the pavement, and taxis hummed by in the distance.

Tiffani finally stopped, hugging her arms lightly.

"I'm sorry," she said softly.

Andre turned to her. "For what?"

"For all of that." She gestured vaguely back toward the lounge. "For Kash… for the drama… for being the reason things are changing between you two."

Andre shook his head. "You not the reason. That was already in him. I just didn't see it."

Tiffani studied his face - the strength in his jawline, the calm in his eyes, the sincerity carved into his expression. Nobody ever looked at her this way. Not as an object, not as a trophy - but as a whole person.

"Still," she whispered. "I didn't want to come between you."

"You didn't," Andre said. "He put himself there. "

Then:

Their eyes held.

Warm.
Heavy.
Undeniably drawn.

Tiffani glanced away, swallowing the heat rising in her chest. "I should probably get home."

"I'll walk you," Andre said - not asking, simply offering, like it was natural.

She hesitated.
A long, charged pause.

Then she nodded.

Walking in the Warm Night

They walked slowly toward her car, the faint glow of the city wrapping them in quiet intimacy.

"So," Andre said after a moment, "What made you really come tonight?"

Tiffani smirked lightly. "Curiosity."

"That's all?"

"And maybe…" She inhaled softly, gathering

courage. "Maybe I wanted to hear you again."

Andre gave a low, soft chuckle. "Hear me?" "Or see me?"

Tiffani tried to hide her smile, but it won anyway. "Both."

Andre stopped walking.

Even the wind paused.

"Tiffani," he said quietly, "Can I tell you something without you running away from me?"

Her pulse jumped. "Maybe. Depends on what it is."

"I wrote something today," he said, pulling out his Notebook. "Didn't know who it was for 'til now."

Tiffani's breath caught.

"Read it," she whispered.

Andre opened the book under the soft streetlight. His voice dropped into that low, smooth tone that had pulled her in from the first moment she heard it.

**"Heaven ain't a place.
Its a moment.
A breath.
A pair of eyes that look at you
like they already know your tomorrow
and still want your today."**

Tiffani's lips parted, heart pounding

Andre stepped slightly closer.

**"Heaven ain't above me.
Ain't past life.
Ain't salvation.
Heaven is the woman
who makes my pulse forget
every heartbreak that came before her name."**

Tiffani exhaled shakily.

He closed the notebook.

"I didn't plan that," he murmured. "Didn't force it. It

just came out… like it was already waiting."

She stared at him - raw emotion flickering behind her eyes. "You can't keep saying things like that."

"Why not?"

"Because…" she took a shaky breath. "Because I feel them."

Andre moved closer, slow enough to give her every chance to pull back.

She didn't.

"Then let yourself feel," he whispered.

Tiffani's voice fell to a whisper. "I've been so careful with my heart…"

"I know." His thumb brushed her cheek, gentle. "I won't break it."

Her eyes fluttered closed, then opened again, full of something soft, something surrendering.

"Andre…" she breathed.

He leaned in.

And she met him halfway.

Their lips touched like flame meeting gasoline, soft at first, then deeper, hungrier, a collision of two souls that had been circling each other for lifetimes. Tiffani's hands slid into his hair. Andre's arms wrapped around her waist, drawing her closer, anchoring her.

It wasn't just a kiss-
I was a beginning.

A dangerous one.

A beautiful one.

When they finally pulled apart, Tiffani's voice trembled.

"I don't want to go home alone tonight."
Andre held her face gently. "You don't have to."

Later That Night - Heaven in the Dark

The city outside blurred into passing lights as they drove to Andre's apartment. Tiffani's hand rested on his thigh; his fingers intertwined with hers. Neither spoke, the silence was hot and full.

Inside, Andre closed the door softly behind them.

Tiffani turned to him, breathing unsteady.

"Say it again," she whispered.

"Say what?"

"Whatever you said in that poem… say something like that again."

Andre stepped toward her slowly, eyes locked onto hers. His voice was deep, velvety, dangerous in the most tender way.

"Your the kind of woman
a man risk sleep for.
Risk peace for.
Risk everything for."

Her knees weakened.

They moved together in a slow, inevitable gravity-kissing again, deeper, fingers exploring, breaths colliding. Clothes slipped away piece by piece. The world dissolved into warmth, mouths, skin, tangled lips, whispered moans.

They made love like they were discovering each other's hidden languages.

Slow.
Passionate.
Explosive.
Sacred.

Tiffani surrendered fully, and Andre treated her

body like she was the poem he'd been trying to write his whole life.

Afterward, she lay against his chest as the room glowed in soft lamplight.

Andre stroked her hair. "You okay?"

She smiled faintly against his skin. "I'm better than okay."

For the first time in years, she felt safe.

Wanted.

Seen.

Cherished.

What neither of them knew now…

Was that this night, this heaven, would soon drag them both into the darkest crossfire of their lives.

Because Kashaka didn't go home.

He didn't sleep.

He didn't calm down.

He spent the night planning.

Watching.

Waiting.

And the love they created tonight….

Would become the very thing he tried to destroy.

CHAPTER SIX - A MAN BECOMING A THREAT

Kashaka didn't go home.

He drove.
Aimlessly at first.
Then with purpose.

Rain glazed the city as he circled block after block, anger boiling in his chest. The windshield wipers thumped a slow rhythm, a heartbeat that didn't belong to him. It only made his thoughts louder.

Tiffani.
Andre.
Together.

His knuckles went white on the steering wheel.

"How he gon' do me like that…" he muttered, voice trembling between rage and heartbreak. "My brother. My day one. He knew how I felt…"

He slammed the heel of his hand against the dashboard.

He should've been the one taking Tiffani home tonight. Not Andre. He'd been there for her for years, walking her to her car at night, helping with security for her boutique, fixing things, listening to her vent.

But she never wanted him.

Because he wasn't Andre.

His mind spiraled, stealing its own oxygen.

"He don't deserve her," he whispered. "He don't even know what to do with a woman like that."

But deep down…
He knew that wasn't true.

Andre was everything Kash wasn't.
Talented.
Magnetic.
Gentle.
Loved.

And now he had the one thing Kashaka had never

been able to reach, Tiffani's heart.

The realization broke something inside him.

Something that wouldn't heal.

Back at Andre's Apartment

The early morning light peeked through Andre's curtains, soft and muted. Tiffani slept curled against him, her breathing calm, her hand resting against his chest.

Andre watched her, peaceful, glowing, even in sleep, and brushed a strand of hair from her face.

There was a gentleness in him that only came out in rare moments. And she had unlocked it without trying.

He kissed her forehead.

She stirred slightly. "Mm… good moring."

"Morning," Andre whispered, smiling.

Tiffani looked up at him, her expression soft but weighed down by reality creeping back in. "Last night was…"

He traced her arm lightly. "Yeah. It was."

She sat up slowly, brushing her curls back. Her voice lowered. "We're going to have to deal with Kash."

Andre sighed, tension settling over his features "I know."

"I don't want anything bad to happen between you two," she murmured.

Andre sat up beside her. "He made his choice. I didn't take anything from him. You're not some prize he owns. You're a grown woman with you own life."

Tiffani leaned against him, but worry lingered in her eyes.

"He didn't look stable last night," she whispered.

Andre's jaw tightened. "I'll talk to him today."

"No," she said quickly, grabbing his arm. "Not yet. Not while he's like this."

Andre looked at her, really looked, and saw fear. Fear for him.

He pulled her close. "Hey. I'm not gonna let anything happen to either of us."

She nodded, but the unease didn't leave her.

Kashaka - Entering the Spiral

Around noon, Kashaka stood in the shadows of an alleyway, staring at Andre's building. He hadn't slept. Hadn't eaten. Hadn't stopped shaking.

    He saw Tiffani leave Andre's apartment building.
Saw her fix her hair.
Saw Andre lean out the window, watching her walk away with the softest smile Kash had ever seen him wear.

The sight made Kash's blood boil.

He stepped back into the alley, gripping the cold metal pipe he'd picked up earlier.

His breathing quickened.

"Okay…" he muttered. "Okay. If that's how he wanna play it…"

He dropped the pipe, ran both hands through his hair, pacing back and forth.

A man walking his dog passed the alley and glanced in curiosity. Kashaka's glare was so venomous the man hurried off.

Kashaka whispered to himself:

"Its not enough to confront him.
He gotta feel what I feel.
He gotta lose her.
He gotta hurt."

His mind snapped into a dangerous clarity.

He pulled out his phone.

Opened a map.
Zoomed into the industrial district.

A place he knew well.

A place nobody checked.

A place with history.

A place with rooms that locked from the outside.

A slow smile crept across his face.

Later That Day - Andre on Edge

    Andre sat on his couch with his guitar resting against his knee, but he couldn't focus on music. Kashaka stalked his thoughts like a storm cloud.

His phone buzzed.

Unknown Number

"We need to talk."

Andre frowned.

Another message popped up immediately.

"Tonight. Alone."

Andre didn't have to guess who it was.

He rose from the couch and grabbed his jacket,
but before he could leave, his phone buzzed again.

This time, it was Tiffani.

Tiffani: Thinking about you.

His expression softened.
Then hardened again, fear creeping in like smoke.

He typed like:

Andre:
Stay close to home tonight, alright? Lock your doors.

Her reply came instantly.

Tiffani:
Why…?

Andre's jaw clenched.

Andre:

Just trust me.

He didn't tell her what he suspected.

He didn't tell her Kashaka had snapped.

He didn't tell her that the man he used to call

brother might soon become his enemy.

The First Step of the Plan

That night, Tiffani closed her boutique later than usual. She doubled-checked the locks, breathed out

a long sigh, an walked toward the parking lot.

She didn't notice the van parked two rows over.
She didn't notice the figure watching her.
She didn't notice the shadow moving silently
Behind her.

She reached her car.

Unlocked it.

And before she cold open the door-

A strong arm wrapped around her waist.
A hand covered her mouth.
Her scream was muffled.

Her purse hit the ground.

Tiffany kicked, fought, clawed, but the man was too strong.

Too familiar.

Kashaka's voice growled in her ear.

"I told you…
You should've picked me."

Everything went black.

CHAPTER SEVEN - THE CITY WITHOUT HER

Andre felt it the moment it happened.

Not the details.
Not the truth.

But the shift.

Something in the air went wrong.

He didn't know why- he just suddenly felt like he needed to call Tiffani, hear her voice, hear her say she was home safe. He pulled his phone from his pocket and dialed her number.

One ring.
Two rings.
Five rings.
Voicemail.

He frowned.

"Tiffani, its me. Call me back."

He hung up, waited, pacing the floor.

Called again.

Voicemail.

"Andre?"
A neighbor poked her head into the hallway as Andre stepped out of his apartment. "You okay, sweetheart.?"

He forced a smile. "Yeah, yes ma'am. Just need to check on somebody."

But on the inside, his stomach twisted.

He tried one more time.

Voicemail.

He swore under his breath and headed for the Stairs.

Her Boutique - Silent

Ten minutes later Andre pulled into the boutique parking lot, his headlights slicing across the empty spaces.

Tiffani's car was there.
But she was not.

"Damn it," he muttered, jumping out of his truck.

The boutique lights were off.
The street was quiet.
Too quiet.

Andre crouched down and scanned beneath her car - checking for movement, anything at all.

Nothing.

But then he spotted something glinting faintly under a sodium streetlamp.

A cellphone.

He rushed to it, snatching it up.

Tiffani's screen was cracked, her wallpaper smiling back at him.

He felt his chest tighten.

This wasn't like her.
Tiffani wouldn't leave without her phone.
She wouldn't vanish.

He picked up her purse next- tossed to the side

Of the parking space like trash.

Panic set in, heavy and suffocating.

He forced himself to breathe through it. "Okay. okay…think."

He looked around.

That's when he noticed tire marks - fresh ones - Cutting through the parking lot and leading toward the street.

A black van had been parked here.

Recently.

And someone had been waiting.

Andre's Call

He dialed Kashaka's number.

Straight to voicemail.

"Yo, Kash, have you seen Tiffani? Call me back as soon as you get this."

He hung up.

A moment passed.

Then he dialed again.

Voicemail.

His pulse quickened. Fear turned to suspicion. Suspicion turned to dread.

He stared at the dark phone screen in his hand, whispering under his breath:

"Kash… what did you do?"

Inside the warehouse

Tiffani awoke to a pounding headache and the smell of old metal.

Her eyes fluttered open.

She was tied to a chair.
Her wrist bound tight.
Her ankles taped together.

A single dim bulb swung overhead.

A cold warehouse surrounded her - concrete walls, rusted beams, shadows that moved with the flicker of the light.

Her breath trembled as she whispered, "Where am I…?"

Footsteps echoed.

Slow.

Heavy.

Coming closer.

She looked up.

Kashaka stepped from the shadows.

But it wasn't the Kashaka she knew.

His eyes were wild.

Red.

Broken.

Full of rage that had rotted him from the inside.

"Kash…" she whispered. "What are you doing? Let me go."

He crouched in front of her, grabbing her chin with trembling fingers. "I loved you, Tiff. You hear me?" "I loved you. And you couldn't see it."

"I never wanted to hurt you -"

"Yeah," he cut her off sharply. "But you hurt me Anyway."

Tiffani swallowed hard, fear rising like a cold tide. "Kash, please… you don't have to do this."

Kashaka stood pacing in circles. "Yeah I do. He took you from me. Andre took everything from me."

Her heart dropped.

Andre.

This was about him.

She shook her head furiously. "Kash, listen. Andre didn't take anything. I made my own choices. I picked who I wanted. You can't punish him for that -"

Kash grabbed her face again, harsh. "Watch me."

Andre - Chasing a Ghost Trail

Andre sped down the main strip, searching every corner, every alley, every street camera he passed. He made calls - friends, drivers, club security, anyone with eyes.

Nothing.

He slammed the heel of his hand against the steering wheel. "Come on, Tiffani. Give me something."

That's when he noticed something in his rearview mirror - a small black dome camera perched

above the boutique parking lot's entrance.

He threw the truck into park and sprinted toward it.

The security system was locked behind a metal panel.

But he knew the owner.
Tifani did business with him all the time.

Andre pounded on the door to the small office next to the boutique.

After a minute, a sleepy older man cracked it open. "Andre? Son, its one in the morning - What's wrong?"

"I need your cameras. Now!! Tiffani's missing."

The owner's face went pale. "Come inside."

The Footage

Seconds later they were staring at grainy black- And - white footage.

Tiffani locking up her boutique.
Walking to her car.
Pausing.
Looking around.

Then- from the corner of the frame - a figure moved fast.

Tiffani disappeared from the screen.

Then a van door slammed.

The vehicle sped away.

Andre leaned in closer.

He froze.

He recognized the silhouette.

The walk.

The shoulders.

The jacket.

"..Kash.."

His voice cracked around the name.

It was like something ripped out of him - like a piece of his heart had been pulled through his chest.

The owner whispered, "You know this man?"

Andre swallowed hard. "Yeah…I know him. "

He backed away slowly, breathing fast.

The fear was gone now.

Replaced with fire.

"With or without help," Andre murmured, " I'm getting her back."

Tiffani - A Promise

Back in the warehouse, Tiffani stared at Kashaka through tears she refused to let fall.

"You're not a killer, Kash."

He laughed - a hollow sound. "Maybe I wasn't."

Tiffani shook her head. "Andre will come for me."

Kashaka stopped pacing.

Turned slowly.

And smiled in a way that chilled her blood.

"I'm counting on it."

Andre- Preparing for war

Andre drove home fast - too fast - and rushed inside his apartment.

He grabbed:

* his crowbar

* his flashlight

* his pocketknife

* and the one thing he hoped he wouldn't have to use - the old pistol he kept locked away since his father died.

His reflection caught in the mirror.

Behind his eyes was something new.
Something stronger than fear.
Stronger than love.

Determination.
Rage.
Hope.

Desperation.

A man ready to burn the whole city down if it meant bringing her home.

He holstered the gun, zipped his jacket, and whispered:

"Hold on, Tiffani. Just hold on for me."

He stepped outside.

And disappeared into the night.

CHAPTER EIGHT - HUNTING IN THE DARK

The city looked different when Andre drove through it with purpose.

Every streetlight felt sharper.
Every shadow felt alive.
Every passing car felt like a threat or a clue.

Andre didn't feel fear anymore - only a brutal, focused calm. The kind a man gets when everything he loves is at stake.

He rolled down the window, letting the cold air hit his face, keeping his senses awake. He gripped the steering wheel tight, knuckles pale.

"Kash…" he muttered.
"You crossed a line you can't come back from."

The Streets Talk

Andre knew where to start.

The industrial district was too big to search blind -
He needed information.
And there was one place where people always knew something:

The Paper Moon

A dive spot where ex- cons, hustlers, mechanics, and night workers hung out. Kashaka had pulled side jobs here before - sometimes legit, sometimes not.

Andre parked outside, pushed the door open, and stepped inside.

Music boomed.
Voices roared.
A haze of smoke floated in the air.

Heads turned when they saw him.

Andre wasn't the type who normally came here.

He walked straight to the bar.

"Yo," the bartender grunted wiping a glass. "You lost, singer boy?"

Andre wasn't in the mood. He slammed a folded hundred on the couter. "I'm looking for Kashaka."

The bartender paused.

A couple men nearby looked up.

Andre leaned in, voice sharpened. "He kidnapped my girl. I'm not leaving without something."

Silence spread like a stain.

One of the men at the back - a heavyset guy with gold teeth - finally spoke. "Kash been actin' real Strange lately. Talkin' bout loyalty, betrayal… all that crazy mess."

Andre stared him down. "You seen him tonight?"

The gold-tooth man scratched his beard. "He came through here earlier. Picked up some bolt cutters from the back. Asked about abandoned buildings in the district."

Andre's stomach tightened. "Which one?"

The man shrugged. "Could be any of 'em. But if he wanted a place no one checks…" He leaned back. "Probably them old textile warehouses by the river. - Building 39, 40, 41. They still got locked rooms, old generators. Real quiet."

Andre's pulse quickened.

"Thank you," he said.

The man waved him off. "Yo, Andre… You goin'

After him alone?"

Andre headed for the door. "I'm not leaving her with him another minute."

Back in the Warehouse - Kash Slipping Further

Tiffani's arms were numb from the ropes.

Her throat was raw from crying.

But she refused to break.

She watched Kash pace back and forth, muttering to himself. The light bulb above him flickered like it couldn't stand his madness either.

"Kashaka", she whispered softly. "Please…listen to me."

He turned sharply.

His eyes were red.

His breathing harsh.

He looked like a man cracked down the middle.

"You don't get it," he said. " I did everything for you."
"YEARS, Tiff.!! I waited. I held you down. I protected you. You never saw me."

"I did see you," she whispered. "As a friend-"

He shouted, voice echoing violently off the walls.
"I didn't want to be no damn FRIEND!"

Tiffani flinched.

He froze, realizing he scared her.

He dropped his voice to a shaking whisper.

"I wanted to be your man…"

Tiffani swallowed, tears building. "Hurting me won't change that. Hurting Andre won't fix it. You know that."

But Kashaka was unraveling thread by thread.

His voice softened into something eerily calm. "He ain't takin' you from me, Tiff. I won't let him."

He walked toward her, brushing her cheek with the back of his hand. She jerked away.

He stiffened - offended.

"You gonna see me," he murmured. "One way or another."

Andre - Following the Trail

Andre sped toward the river district, passing warehouses long abandoned, their windows broken, their signage faded.

As he turned onto a cracked access road, his headlights illuminated a rusted metal sign:

WAREHOUSE COMPLEXES 39 - 41

His heart pounded.

He slowed the truck, scanning the surroundings.

Nothing but silence.
Black buildings.
And the hum of faraway machinery.

He moved like a shadow -quiet, controlled.

Every instinct screamed Tiffani's name.

He approached **Warehouse 39** first.

Locked.

Windows boarded shut.

He checked **40** next.

The chain on the door hung broken - freshly cut.

Andre touched the metal

Cold.

Sharp.

Recent.

His jaw clenched.

"He's here."

He reached into his jacket and pulled out the pistol.

Not for intimidation.

For survival.

He took a breath.

Slipped inside.

Tiffani - Beginning to Resist

Kashaka was rummaging through a metal cabinet across the room, looking for something. Tools clanged. A drawer slammed.

Tiffani tested the ropes at her wrists - twisting, pulling, trying to loosen them without making Noise,

Her skin burned.

Her fingers ached.

But the knot budged - just a little.

She kept working it, breathing quietly through the pain.

Kash…please don't turn around.

Andre - Inside the Maze

The warehouse was almost pitch black, lit only by

Andre's flashlight beam curring through layers of dust.

He stepped carefully over broken pallets and old chains.

Water dripped somewhere in the distance.

His flashlight landed on footprints in the dust - two sets.

One light.
One heavier.

He followed them deeper.

His breath trembled when he saw something ahead:

Tiffani's bracelet.

Broken. On the floor.

He bent down, touching it like a sacred thing.

"Tiff…" he whispered.

Then he heard a scream.

Muffled.

Muffled, but hers.

Andre bolted toward the sound.

Kashaka's Breaking Point

Tiffani finally loosened one wrist - just enough to slip her hand through if she turned it carefully.

Her heart raced.

But before she could finish freeing herself - Kash slammed the drawer shut and turned around.

He froze.

Stared at her.

And his face twisted with rage.

"You trynna run from me?" he snarled, stepping toward her.

Tiffani shook her head quickly, fear surging. "Kash -wait-"

He reached toward her gripping her shoulders -

A loud bang echoed through the warehouse.

Kashaka stopped.

Tiffani's eyes widened

Andre's voice carried from the hallway:

"KASHAKA! LET HER GO!!"

Kash's jaw tightened.
His breath grew jagged.
He slowly turned toward the doorway.

His voice was deadly quiet."Right on Time."

CHAPTER NINE - BROTHERS TURNED ENEMIES

Andre stepped into the warehouse with the pistol raised, flashlight beam slicing through the dark like A blade. His heartbeat was loud in his ears - not from fear, but from fury.

Tiffany saw him first.

"Andre!" she cried, voice tight with terror.

Her hands were still halfway bound. She struggled against the ropes, desperate to reach him.

Kashaka stood between them, shoulders squared, face twisted with something past anger - something wounded, betrayed, feral.

Andre aimed the gun squarely at him.

"Kash," he said, voice low, shaking with emotion. "Move away from her."

Kashaka smiled.
A slow broken smile that didn't reach his eyes.

"Oh, so now you wanna talk, huh?"

"Kash, I'm serious," Andre snapped. " Back. Up."

But Kashaka didn't move.
Didn't flinch.
Didn't blink.

Instead he stepped closer to Tiffani, placing a hand on the back of her chair.

Tiffani stiffened in fear.
"Andre," Kash said softly, "you came for her. Just like I knew you would."

Andre's grip on the pistol tightened. "Let her go. This doesn't end with you dying tonight. Don't

make that choice."

Kashaka laughed- a raw, hoarse sound that echoed off the metal beams.

"Die?" he muttered. " You think I care about that?"
Andre shook his head. "Man you're not thinking

straight -"

"Oh, I'm thinking perfectly clear." Kashaka hissed. "I been clear for years, Andre. Clearer than you!" He jabbed a finger at his own temple. " I watched you take everything I ever wanted."

Andre's voice cracked. "I never took anything from you -"

"You took her!" Kash roared, slamming nis fist into The chair so hard Tiffani yelped and flinched. "You Took the one damn thing that kept me alive in this world!"

Tiffani's voice trembled.
"Kash…please stop. I don't want you to get hurt."

Kashaka turned to her, eyes softening for a split second.

Then hardening again.

"I didn't wanna hurt you, Tiff," he whispered. "But he left me no choice."

Andre stepped forward.

gun still raised,

voice controlled but shaking.

"Kash, you're my brother," he said. "We been through everything. Don't do this. This ain't you."

Kashaka slowly turned back to Andre.

"I was your brother," he corrected. "Before you stole the only woman I ever loved."

Andre swallowed hard. "She chose me, Kash. You can't force someone to love you. You kow that."

Kashaka's jaw clenched so hard it shook.

A long silence filled the warehouse.

Then Kash lifted his chin.
A decision made.

"You know what?" he whispered.

"Let's settle this like men."

He kicked the chair - sending Tiffani crashing sideways onto the concrete.

"Andre!!" she cried out.

Andre surged forward, rage exploding through him. But Kashaka was fast - he grabbed a metal pipe from the floor and swung it at Andre's head. Andre ducked, the pipe whistling inches above him.

Andre shoved Kash hard, the gun flying from his grip and skidding across the floor.

It was gone - swallowed by darkness.

Now it was just fists.

The Fight Begins

Kashaka charged.

Andre met him halfway, slamming a fist into Kash's jaw. Kash staggered - then grinned, blood already on his lip.

"You hit like you sing," Kash spat.
"Soft."
Andre's fist crashed into his face again.

"Try me again," Andre growled.

Kash roared and tackled Andre, slamming him into a stack of wooden pallets. The impact rattled Andre's spine, but he kicked Kash off and rolled to his feet.

The two men circled each other, breathing hard,
Sweat shining in the dim flickering light.

Kash's knuckles were split.
Andre's cheek was bleeding.
Their friendship lay shattered between them like glass.

"You always had everything," Kash snarled.
"The talent. The charm. The women. The love. And I got scraps."

Andre spit blood out on the floor.
"You had me," he said quietly.

For a moment - just a moment - Kash flinched.

Then his expression twisted again.

He charged.

Andre dodged left - too slow - Kash's fist slammed into his ribs so hard he folded. Air left his lungs in a violent exhale.

Tiffani screamed from the floor, "Andre! Get up! Please!"

He did.

He always did.

Andre raised his fist again.

Tiffani - Desperation turning to Action

    Tiffani had managed to free one wrist. The rope burned her skin raw, she didn't care.

She tugged harder.

Harder.

Her other wrist slipped free.

She gasped - not in relief, but with renewed terror. Andre was losing ground.

Kashaka slammed Andre into a support beam. Andre's head cracked back against it, dazing him.

Tiffani crawled across the floor toward the fallen pistol, hand shaking violently.

Kashaka didn't see her.

He grabbed Andre by the collar and threw him across the room.

"Andre!" she cried.

He hit the floor hard- but rolled, breathing in ragged pants.

Kash stalked toward him, pipe raised again.

"Should've stayed away from her," he growled.

Tiffani's fingers closed around the pistol.

She aimed it with both hands.

"Kashaka," she whispered, voice trembling.

He turned.

And froze.

"Tiff… put that down."

"No," she said, tears streaming.
"You're not hurting him anymore."

The Breaking Point

Andre struggled to his feet, wiping blood from the corner of his mouth.

Kashaka stared at them -his oldest friend, bruised and exhausted… and the woman he loved pointing a gun at him.

His expression collapsed.

"You really choose him… over me?"

Tiffani whispered, "I didn't choose him over you. I chose him because he loved me right."

Something shattered inside of Kashaka's chest.

He screamed - a raw, agonized sound - and charged at Andre one more time.

Andre met him head-on.

They collided in a brutal clash of fist, elbows, knees - years of brotherhood exploding into violence.

Andre slammed Kash into the ground.
Kash rolled and punched Andre across the face.
Andre kneed him in the stomach.
Kash headbutted him - dazed him - tried to reach for the gun in Tiffani's hand.

But she stepped back, shaking, keeping it aimed.

"Kash, STOP!" she yelled.

But he didn't.
He lunged at her.

Andre grabbed him from behind dragging him down.

The two men hit the ground hard, wrestling in the dust, grunting, choking, punching - fighting for far more than survival.

Fighting for heartbreak.

Fighting for betrayal.

Fighting for love.

And then-

A single gunshot echoed.

The whole warehouse went still.

Andre froze.

Kash froze.

Tiffani froze.

Smoke curled from the pistol barrel in Tiffani's trembling hands.

Kashaka slowly looked down.

Blood began spreading across his shirt…
just above his ribs.

His knees buckled.

Andre caught him before he hit the ground.

"Kash!" Andre shouted, lowering him gently. "Kash!! Stay with me! Don't you dare-"

Kash stared up at him, eyes dazed, lips trembling.

"Andre…" he whispered. "I didn't… I never wanted…".

Blood bubbled at the corner of his mouth.

Andre's voice broke. "Why'd you make me do this, Man? Why!?"

Kash tried to speak - but the words died in his throat.

His eyes drifted…
Then dimmed.

Andre felt the weight go out0 of his body.

The room spun.

Tiffani sobbed into her hands.

　　Andre leaned over Kashaka's body, fist pressed to his forehead, tears mixing with the blood on the concrete.

His brother was gone.
The battle was over.
But the price… was devastating.

Made in the USA
Coppell, TX
30 January 2026

70526830R00057